W9-BYA-992

# by Erin Soderberg
## Illustrated by Duendes del Sur

**visit us at www.abdopublishing.com**

Reinforced library bound edition published in 2013 by Spotlight, a division of the ABDO Group, PO Box 398166, Minneapolis, MN 55439. Spotlight produces high-quality reinforced library bound editions for schools and libraries. Published by agreement with Warner Bros.-A Time Warner Company.

Printed in the United States of America, North Mankato, Minnesota.
102012
012013

♻ This book contains at least 10% recycled materials.

Cover designed by Madalina Stefan and Mary Hall
Interiors designed by Mary Hall

**Library of Congress Cataloging-in-Publication Data**
*This book was previously cataloged with the following information:*

Soderberg, Erin.
Dinosaur dig / by Erin Soderberg ; illustrated by Duendes del Sur.
p. cm. -- (Scooby-Doo! Picture Clue Books)
Uncle Ted gets Scooby-Doo and his friends to help find dinosaur bones for the museum, but the bones turn up missing. Can Scooby and his friends find the bones?
[1. Rebuses. 2. Dinosaurs--Juvenile fiction. 3. Dogs--Fiction. 4. Mystery and detective stories.]
PZ7.S685257
[E]

00711986

ISBN 978-1-61479-037-2 (reinforced library bound edition)

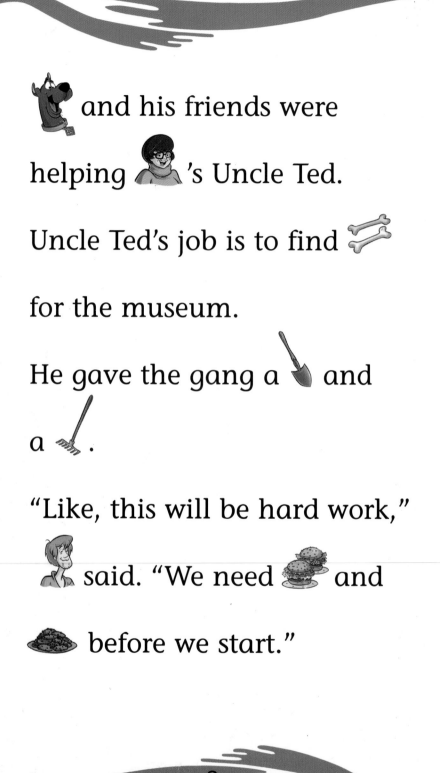 and his friends were

helping 's Uncle Ted.

Uncle Ted's job is to find

for the museum.

He gave the gang a and

a .

"Like, this will be hard work,"

said. "We need and

before we start."

"Have you found any  yet?"

 asked.

"Look in that ," Uncle Ted

said.

 looked. The  was empty.

"Oh, no!" Uncle Ted shouted.

"All the  are gone."

"Maybe there's a  ghost hiding all the 🦴!" 🧍 said.

"Roh, no!" said 🐕.

"We have to help Uncle Ted find the missing 🦴," 👩 said.

"He needs the 🦴 for the museum," 👧 said.

"Let's look for clues, gang!" said 👦.

and looked for clues.

They found a food .

"Let's check the ,"

Shaggy said.

They found some and .

But they did not find the

missing .

"Jinkies!"  said.

She found a big 🍔 in a ⬛.

But there were no 🦴.

🧑 and 👧 found a 🪣.

But they did not find the 🦴.

"Well, gang," Uncle Ted said.

"Let's make a . We can look

for the in the morning."

Uncle Ted made .

Then the gang roasted over

the .

"Like, I hope the ghost does

not like ," said.

"Did you hear that noise?"  asked.

"  , let's go check it out," said.

 jumped into the .

"Would you do it for a ?" asked.

Oh, no! All the were gone!

Did the  ghost take the ?

wanted to find the .

"Come on, gang," said.

Maybe they would find the .

Hopefully they would not find the ghost!

The  helped  and the

gang to see in the dark.

 used his nose to search for

the  and the 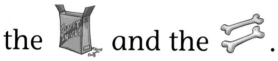.

They looked in a 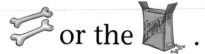.

They found Uncle Ted's ![dog].

But they did not find the missing

![bone] or the ![bag of snacks].

 smelled  and wagged

his  .

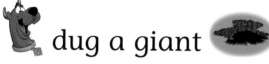 dug a giant  in the dirt

with his paws.

Uncle Ted's  jumped into the

 and pulled out some ✂ .

There was no 🦖 ghost!

"You found the ,  !"
 said.

"You saved the museum's  ,"

Uncle Ted said. "You are a hero!"
 threw  a  .

"Scooby-Dooby-Doo!"  barked.

Did you spot all the picture clues
in this Scooby-Doo mystery?

Reading is fun with Scooby-Doo!